May 2016

Dear Felicity

Welcome to the world and to our neighbourhood. So wonderful to watch you grow!!

Much joy and love

Carol

Silver Bells & Cockle Shells

Illustrated Classic Nursery Rhymes

Illustrated by Henriëtte Willebeek Le Mair

Floris Books

Contents

Pussy Cat, Pussy Cat

"Pussy Cat, Pussy Cat, where have you been?"
  "I've been up to London to visit the Queen."
"Pussy Cat, Pussy Cat, what did you there?"
  "I frightened a little mouse, under her chair."

Mary Had a Little Lamb

Mary had a little lamb
  Its fleece was white as snow,
And everywhere that Mary went
  The lamb was sure to go.
He followed her to school one day,
  That was against the rule;
It made the children laugh and play
  To see a lamb at school.

So the teacher turned him out
  But still he lingered near,
And waited patiently about
  Till Mary did appear;
And then he ran to her and laid
  His head upon her arm,
As if he said, "I'm not afraid:
  You'll keep me from all harm."

"What makes the lamb love Mary so?"
  The eager children cry.
"Oh, Mary loves the lamb you know,"
  The teacher did reply;
"And you each gentle animal
  In confidence may bind
And make them follow at your call
  If you are always kind."

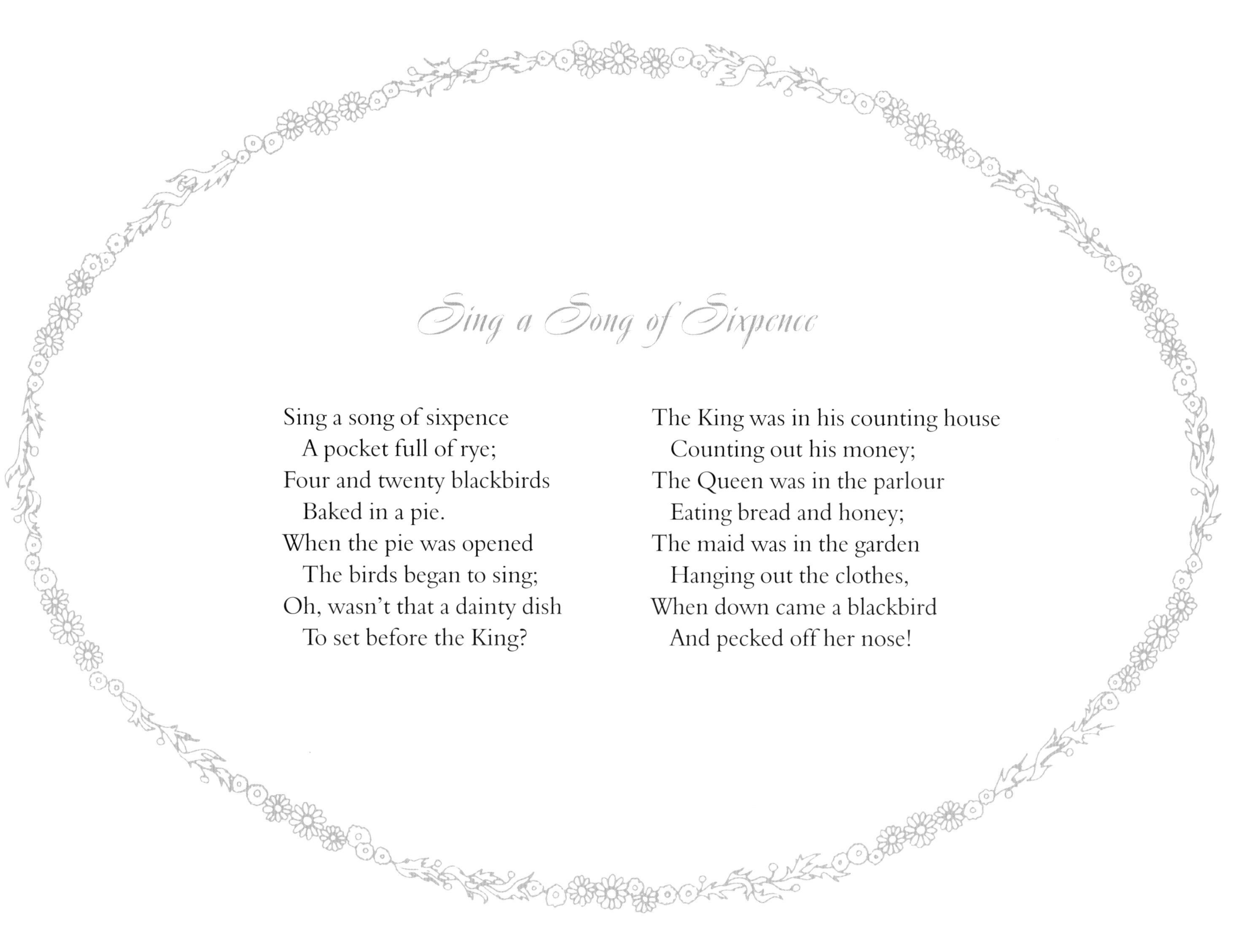

Sing a Song of Sixpence

Sing a song of sixpence
  A pocket full of rye;
Four and twenty blackbirds
  Baked in a pie.
When the pie was opened
  The birds began to sing;
Oh, wasn't that a dainty dish
  To set before the King?

The King was in his counting house
  Counting out his money;
The Queen was in the parlour
  Eating bread and honey;
The maid was in the garden
  Hanging out the clothes,
When down came a blackbird
  And pecked off her nose!

Little Jack Horner

Little Jack Horner
   Sat in a corner
Eating his Christmas pie.
   He put in his thumb
And pulled out a plum
   And said, “What a good boy am I!”

Ding Dong Bell

Ding dong bell!
  Pussy's in the well!
Who put her in?
  Little Johnny Flynn.
Who pulled her out?
  Little Tommy Stout.
What a naughty boy was that
  To try to drown poor pussy cat,
Who ne'er did him any harm,
  But killed all the mice in farmer's barn.

Three Blind Mice

Three blind mice! Three blind mice!
See how they run! See how they run!
They all ran after the farmer's wife,
Who cut off their tails with a carving knife.
Did you ever see such a thing in your life,
As three blind mice!

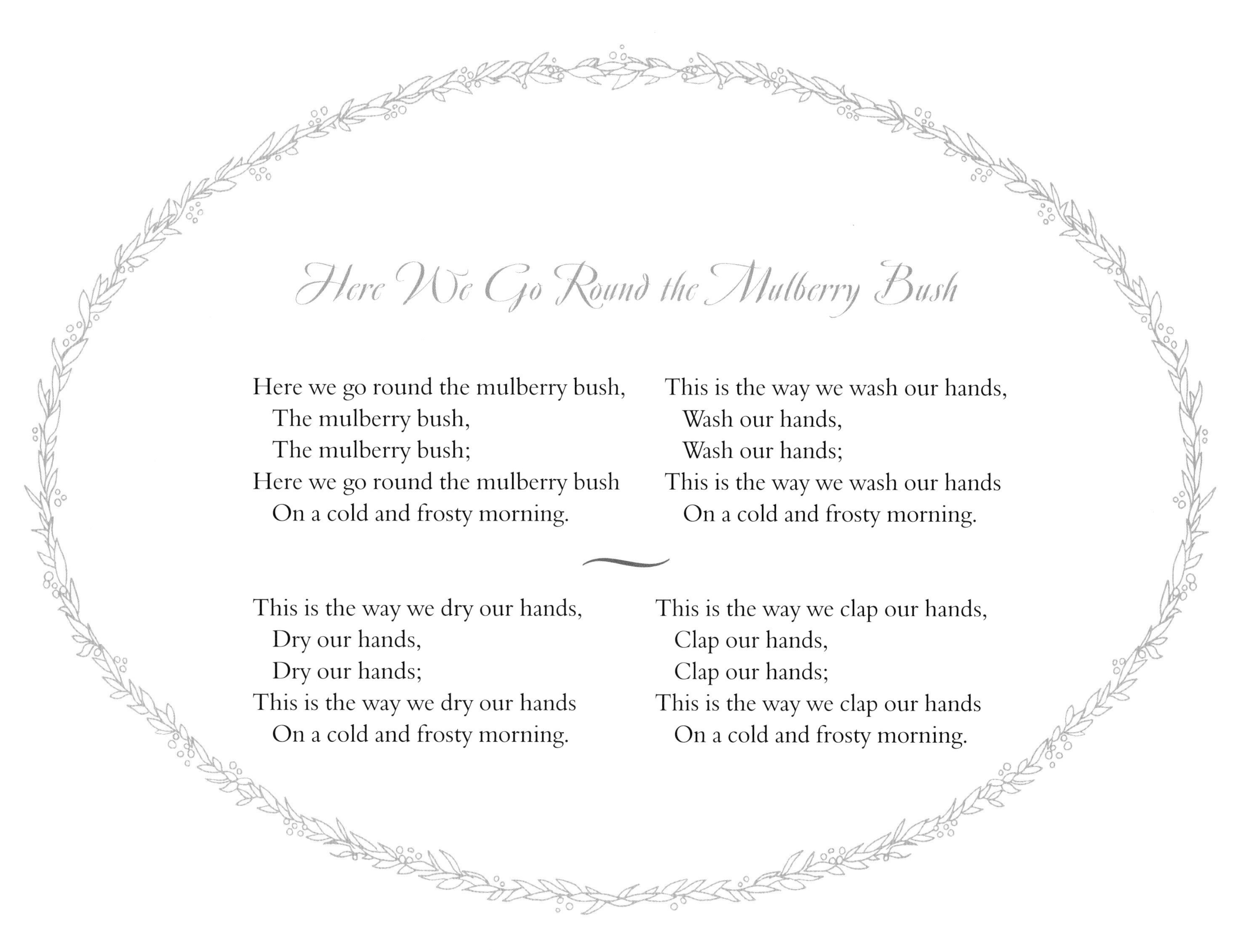

Here We Go Round the Mulberry Bush

Here we go round the mulberry bush,
The mulberry bush,
The mulberry bush;
Here we go round the mulberry bush
On a cold and frosty morning.

This is the way we wash our hands,
Wash our hands,
Wash our hands;
This is the way we wash our hands
On a cold and frosty morning.

This is the way we dry our hands,
Dry our hands,
Dry our hands;
This is the way we dry our hands
On a cold and frosty morning.

This is the way we clap our hands,
Clap our hands,
Clap our hands;
This is the way we clap our hands
On a cold and frosty morning.

Three Little Kittens

Three little kittens,
they lost their mittens
And they began to cry,
"Oh, Mother dear! We sadly fear,
Our mittens we have lost."
"What! Lost your mittens?
You naughty kittens,
Then you shall have no pie."
"Mee-ow, mee-ow,
We shall have no pie."

The three little kittens,
they found their mittens
And they began to shout,
"Oh, Mother dear! See here, see here!
Our mittens we have found."
"What! Found your mittens?
You good little kittens,
Then you shall have some pie."
"Purr, purr, purr, purr,
We shall have some pie."

The three little kittens, they washed their mittens
And hung them up to dry;
"Oh, Mother dear! Do you not hear,
Our mittens we have washed!"
"What! Washed your mittens, then you're good kittens,
I smell a rat close by."
"Mee-ow, mee-ow,
We smell a rat close by."

Pat-a-Cake

Pat-a-cake, pat-a-cake, baker's man!
  Bake me a cake as fast as you can.
Pat it and prick it and mark it with B,
  And put it in the oven for baby and me.
  For baby and me,
  For baby and me,
And put it in the oven for baby and me.

Mary, Mary, Quite Contrary

"Mary, Mary, quite contrary,
How does your garden grow?"
"With silver bells and cockle shells
And pretty maids all in a row."

Lucy Locket

Lucy Locket lost her pocket,
  Kitty Fisher found it,
Not a penny was there in it,
  Only ribbon round it.

I Love Little Pussy

I love little Pussy,
Her coat is so warm;
And if I don't hurt her,
She'll do me no harm.

So I'll not pull her tail,
Or drive her away;
But Pussy and I
Very gently will play.

She will sit by my side
And I'll give her some food;
And Pussy will love me
Because I am good.

I'll pat pretty Pussy,
And then she will purr;
And thus show her thanks
For my kindness to her.

I'll not pinch her ears,
Or tread on her paws,
Lest I should provoke her
To use her sharp claws.

I never will vex her
Nor make her displeased:
For pussies don't like
To be worried and teased.

Baa Baa Black Sheep

"Baa, baa, black sheep,
  Have you any wool?"
"Yes Sir, yes Sir,
  Three bags full:
One for the master,
  And one for the dame,
And one for the little boy
  Who lives down the lane."

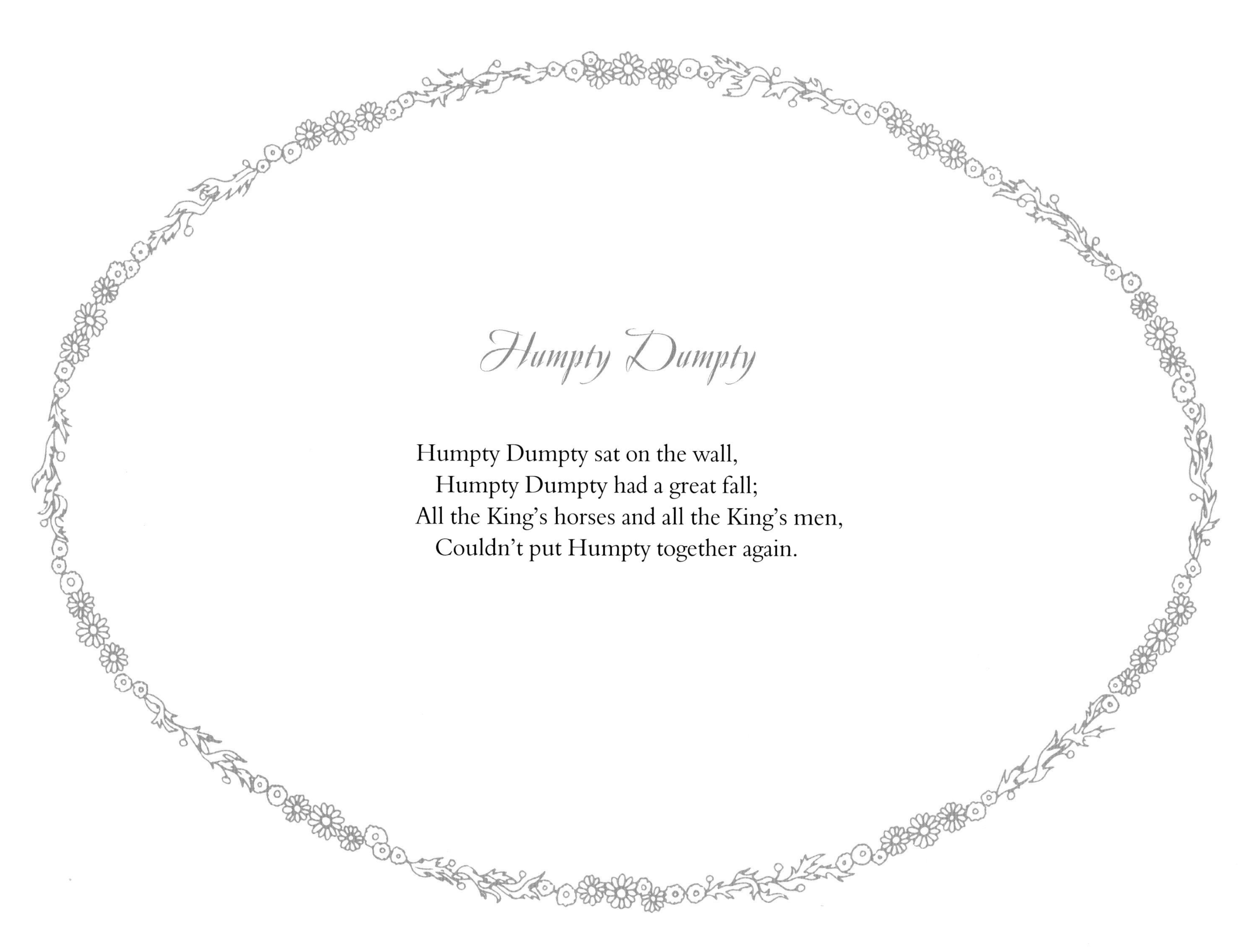

Humpty Dumpty

Humpty Dumpty sat on the wall,
 Humpty Dumpty had a great fall;
All the King's horses and all the King's men,
 Couldn't put Humpty together again.

Oh Where has my Little Dog Gone?

Oh where, oh where has my little dog gone?
  Oh where, oh where can he be?
With his ears cut short and his tail cut long,
  Oh where, oh where can he be?

Georgie Porgie

Georgie Porgie pudding and pie
Kissed the girls and made them cry;
When the boys came out to play
Georgie Porgie ran away.

Little Miss Muffet

Little Miss Muffet
  Sat on a tuffet,
Eating her curds and whey;
  Along came a spider,
Who sat down beside her
  And frightened Miss Muffet away.

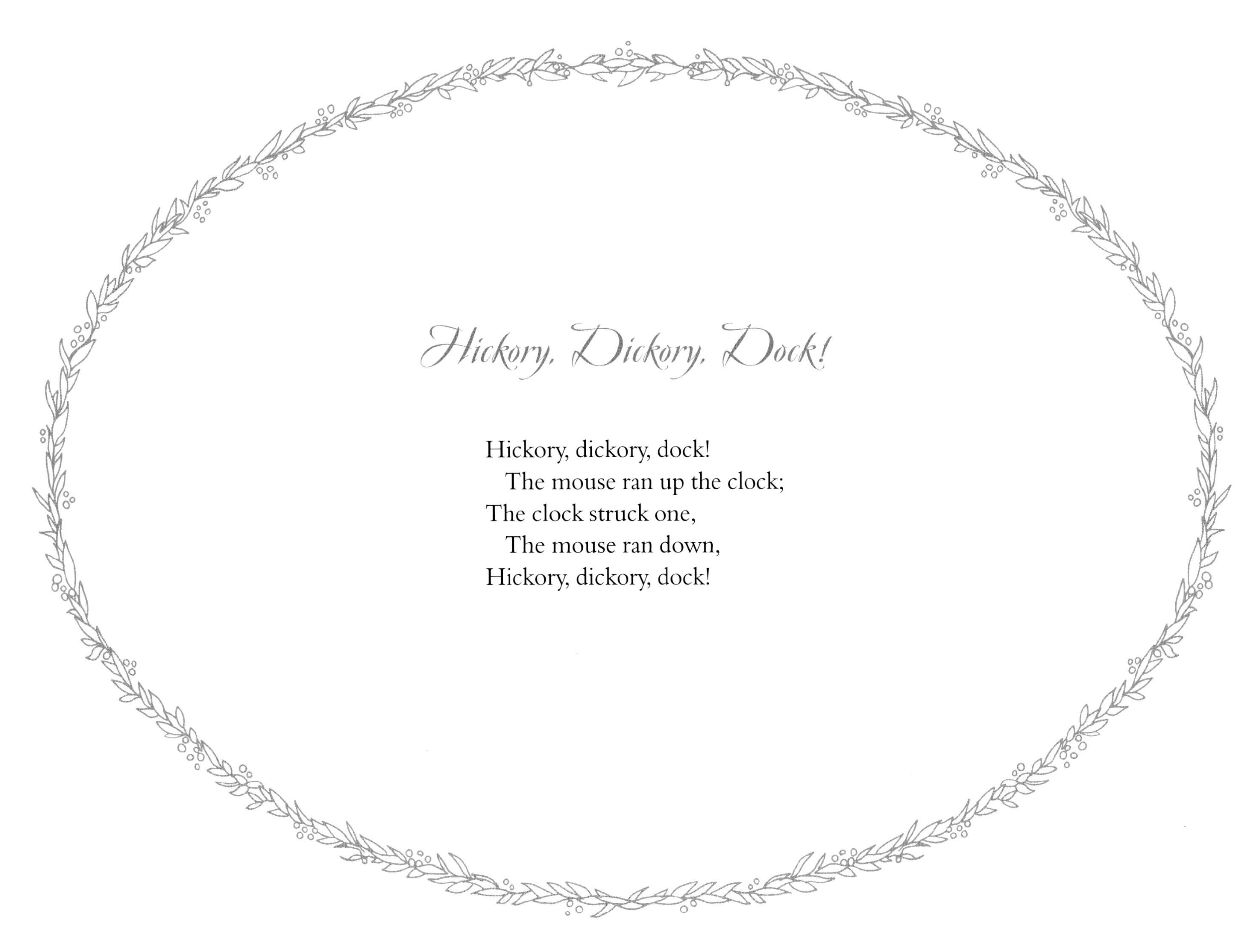

Hickory, Dickory, Dock!

Hickory, dickory, dock!
  The mouse ran up the clock;
The clock struck one,
  The mouse ran down,
Hickory, dickory, dock!

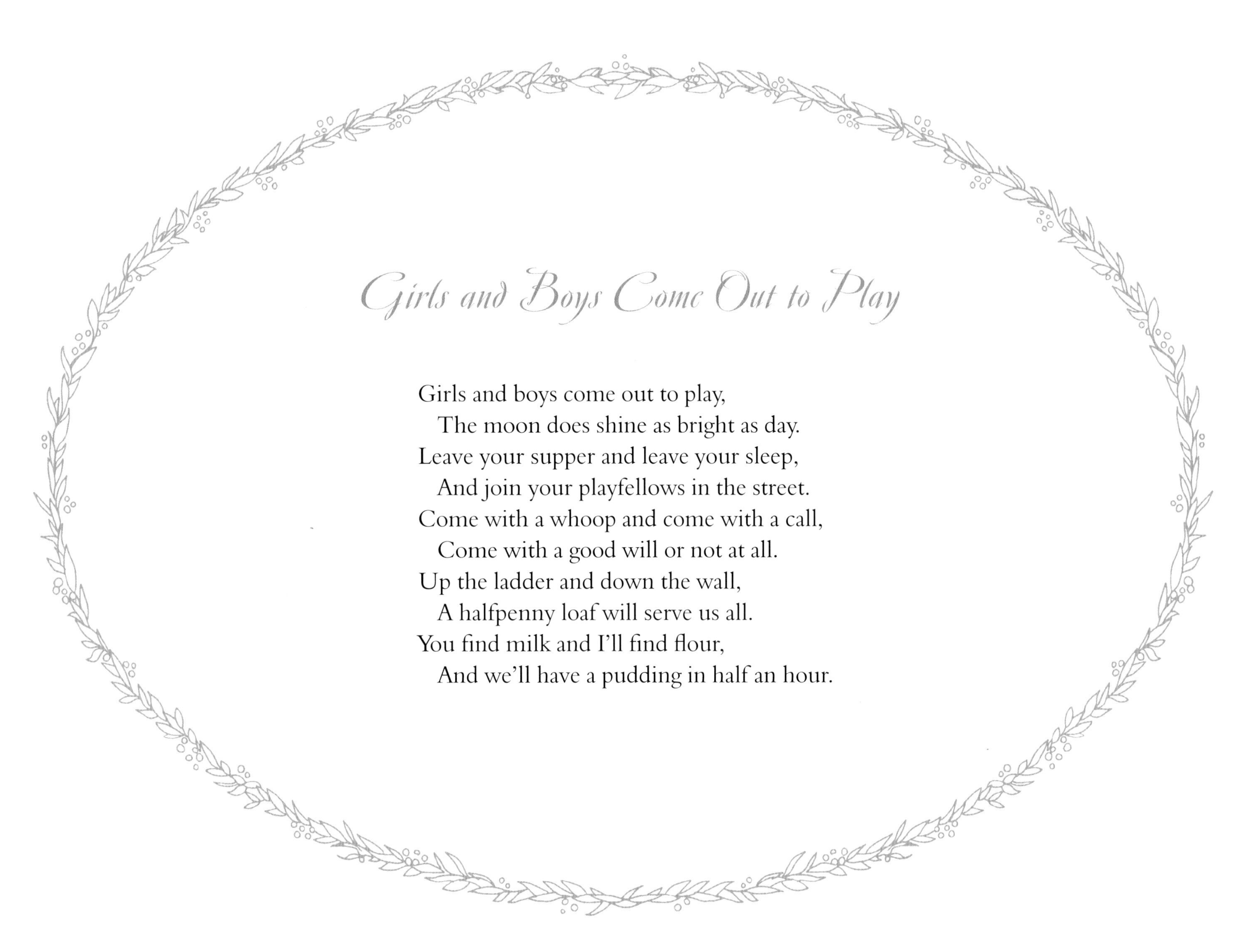

Girls and Boys Come Out to Play

Girls and boys come out to play,
The moon does shine as bright as day.
Leave your supper and leave your sleep,
And join your playfellows in the street.
Come with a whoop and come with a call,
Come with a good will or not at all.
Up the ladder and down the wall,
A halfpenny loaf will serve us all.
You find milk and I'll find flour,
And we'll have a pudding in half an hour.

Jack and Jill

Jack and Jill went up the hill
To fetch a pail of water;
Jack fell down and broke his crown,
And Jill came tumbling after.

Up Jack got, and home did trot,
As fast as he could caper;
He went to bed and bound his head
With vinegar and brown paper.

Yankee Doodle

Yankee Doodle went to town
Riding on a pony,
He stuck a feather in his cap
And called it macaroni.
Yankee Doodle, doodle do,
Yankee Doodle dandy;
All the lassies are so smart
And sweet as sugar candy.

Twinkle, Twinkle, Little Star

Twinkle, twinkle, little star,
How I wonder what you are,
Up above the world so high,
Like a diamond in the sky.
Twinkle, twinkle, little star,
How I wonder what you are.

When the blazing sun is gone,
When he nothing shines upon,
Then you show your little light,
Twinkle, twinkle, all the night.
Twinkle, twinkle, little star,
How I wonder what you are.

Then the traveller in the dark,
Thanks you for your tiny spark;
He could not see which way to go,
If you did not twinkle so.
Twinkle, twinkle, little star,
How I wonder what you are.

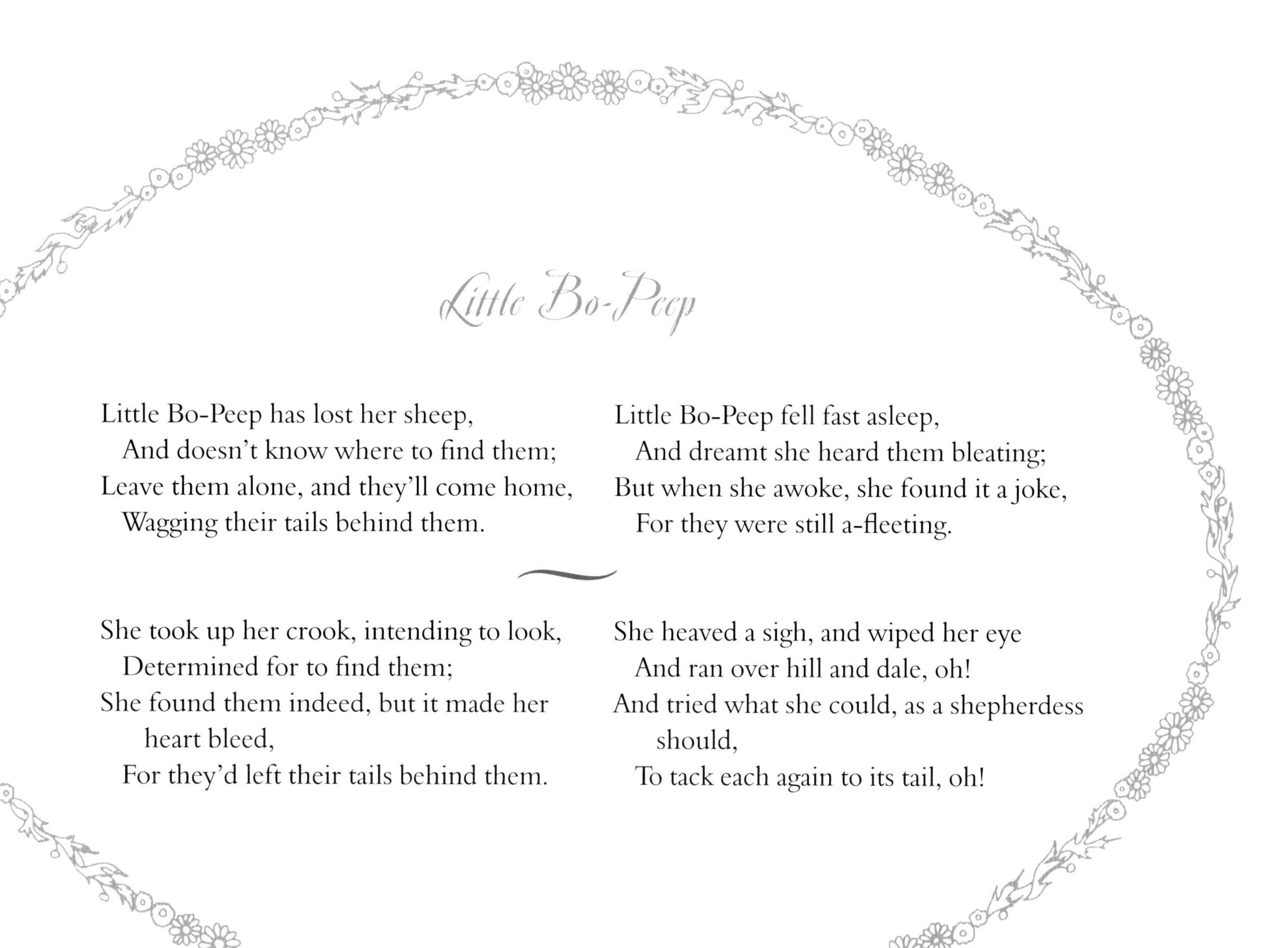

Little Bo-Peep

Little Bo-Peep has lost her sheep,
And doesn't know where to find them;
Leave them alone, and they'll come home,
Wagging their tails behind them.

Little Bo-Peep fell fast asleep,
And dreamt she heard them bleating;
But when she awoke, she found it a joke,
For they were still a-fleeting.

She took up her crook, intending to look,
Determined for to find them;
She found them indeed, but it made her heart bleed,
For they'd left their tails behind them.

She heaved a sigh, and wiped her eye
And ran over hill and dale, oh!
And tried what she could, as a shepherdess should,
To tack each again to its tail, oh!

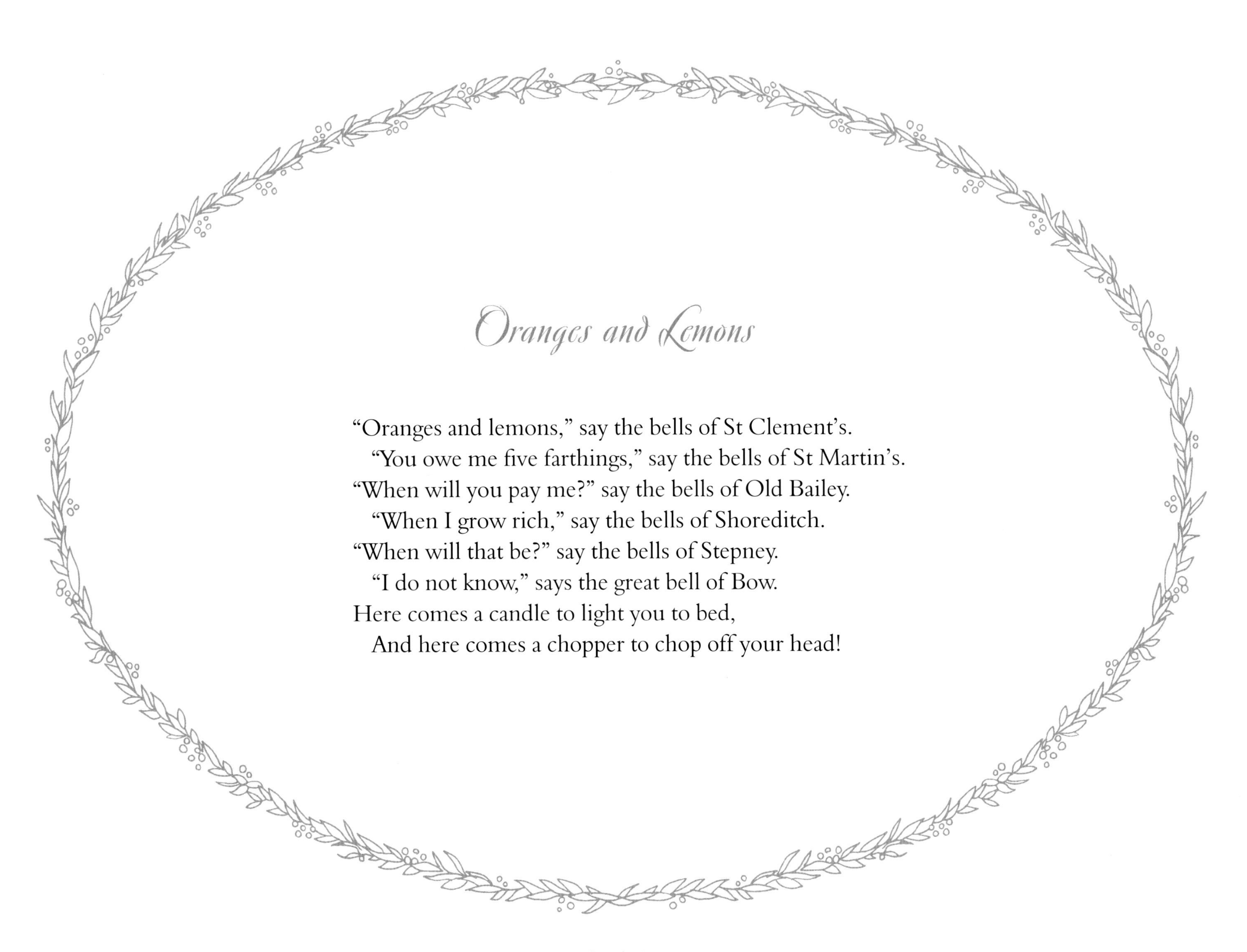

Oranges and Lemons

"Oranges and lemons," say the bells of St Clement's.
"You owe me five farthings," say the bells of St Martin's.
"When will you pay me?" say the bells of Old Bailey.
"When I grow rich," say the bells of Shoreditch.
"When will that be?" say the bells of Stepney.
"I do not know," says the great bell of Bow.
Here comes a candle to light you to bed,
And here comes a chopper to chop off your head!

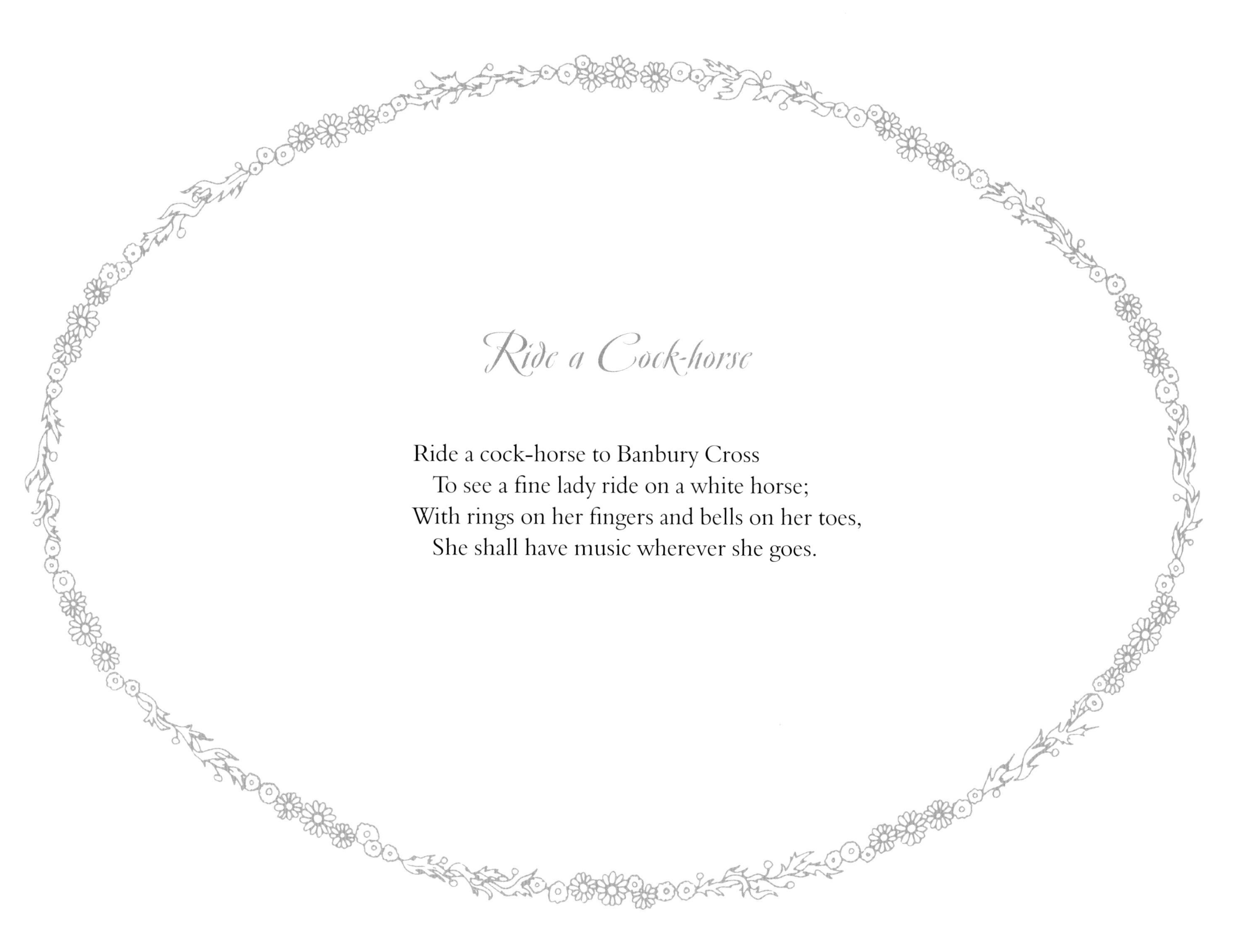

Ride a Cock-horse

Ride a cock-horse to Banbury Cross
  To see a fine lady ride on a white horse;
With rings on her fingers and bells on her toes,
  She shall have music wherever she goes.

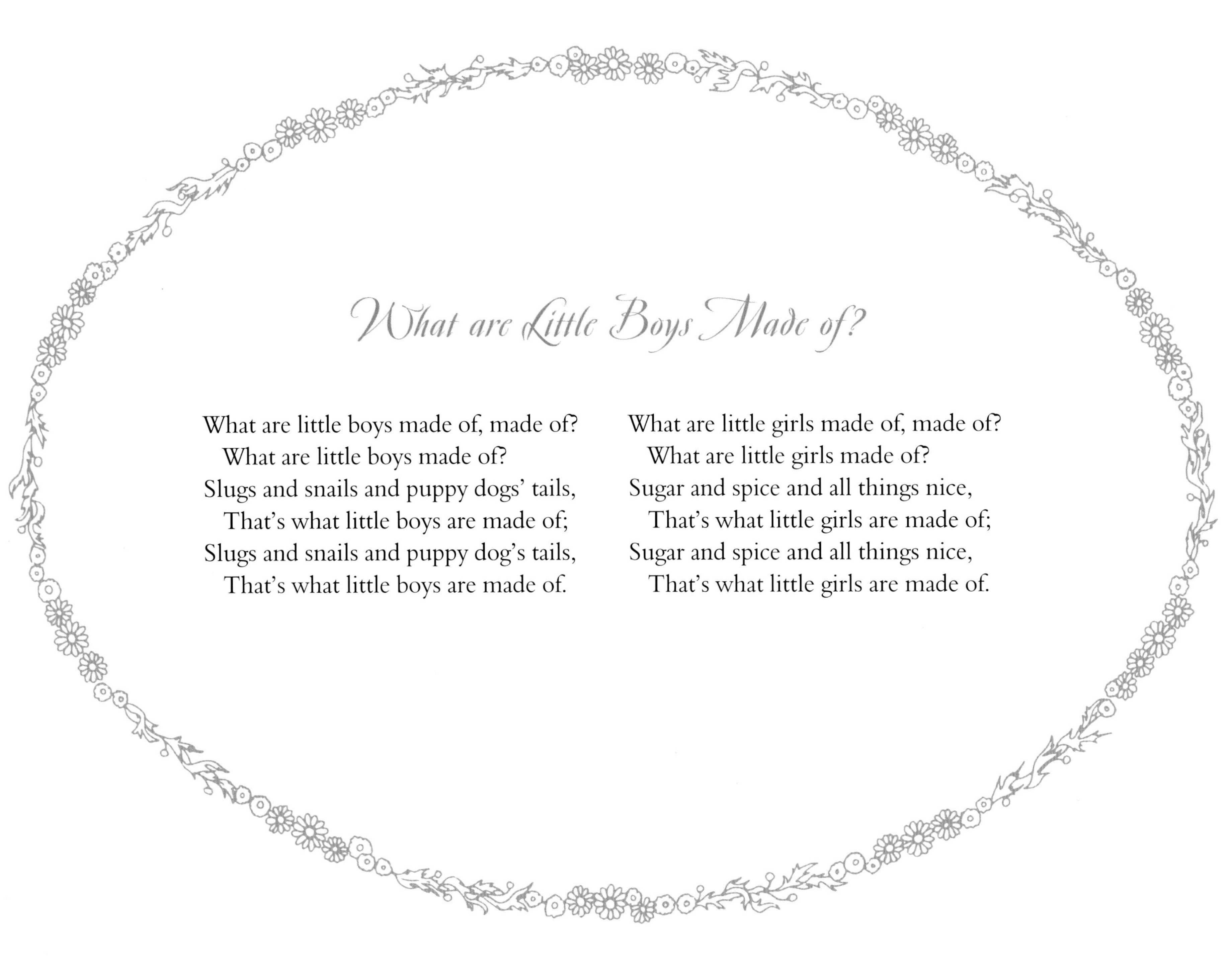

What are Little Boys Made of?

What are little boys made of, made of?
  What are little boys made of?
Slugs and snails and puppy dogs' tails,
  That's what little boys are made of;
Slugs and snails and puppy dog's tails,
  That's what little boys are made of.

What are little girls made of, made of?
  What are little girls made of?
Sugar and spice and all things nice,
  That's what little girls are made of;
Sugar and spice and all things nice,
  That's what little girls are made of.

There was a Little Man

There was a little man,
And he wooed a little maid,
And he said, "Little maid!
Will you wed, wed, wed?
I have little more to say,
Then will you? Yea, or nay!
For least said is soonest mended-ded!"

The little maid replied,
(Some say, a little sighed,)
"But what shall we have to eat, eat, eat?
Will the love that you're so rich in,
Put a fire into the kitchen?
Or the little God of Love
Turn the spit, spit, spit?"

The little man replied,
(Some say, a little cried,
For his heart was filled with sorrow-row);
"With the little that I have,
I will be your little slave,
And the rest my little dear
We will borrow-row."

Thus did the little gent,
Make the little maid relent,
For her little heart began to beat, beat, beat;
Though his offers were but small,
She took them one and all,
Now she thanks her lucky stars
For her fate, fate, fate.

Little Boy Blue

Little Boy Blue, come blow your horn,
  The sheep's in the meadow, the cow's in the corn.
Where's the boy who looks after the sheep?
  He's under the haystack fast asleep.
Will you wake him? No, not I,
  For if I do, he's sure to cry.

Polly Put the Kettle on

Polly put the kettle on,
  Polly put the kettle on,
Polly put the kettle on,
  We'll all have tea.

Sukey take it off again,
  Sukey take it off again,
Sukey take it off again,
  They've all gone away.

Hush-a-bye Baby

Hush-a-bye baby on the treetop,
 When the wind blows the cradle will rock;
When the bough breaks the cradle will fall,
 And down will come baby, cradle and all!

First published as *Our Old Nursery Rhymes* by Augener Ltd in 1911
This edition published by Floris Books in 2013

www.florisbooks.co.uk
British Library CIP data available
ISBN 978-178250-005-6
Printed in Malaysia